There Are Many Great Things You Can Do in the Snow

There Are Many Great Things You Can Do in the Snow

By

Howard Hofherr

Illustrated by

Denise Hofherr-Hevesy

Ozark Publishing, Inc.
P.O. Box 228
Prairie Grove, AR 72753

Library of Congress cataloging-in-publication data

Hofherr, Howard, 1935-
There are many great things you can do in the snow / by
Howard Hofherr ; illustrated by Denise Hofherr.
p. cm.
Summary: When she discovers that school has been canceled, a young girl lies in bed thinking of all the fun she and her friends will have playing in the snow.
ISBN 1-56763-308-0 (alk. paper). — ISBN 1-56763-309-9
(pbk. : alk. paper)
[1. Snow—Fiction. 2. Stories in rhyme.] I. Hofherr-Hevesy,
Denise, 1968-
ill. II. Title.
PZ7.H67865Th 1997
[E]—dc20 96-36275
CIP
AC

Printed in the United States of America

Dedicated to

my wife, Jean; our five children, Bob, Bill, Rich, Denise (who illustrated the book), and Donna (who starred in it); and to our ten grandchildren.

She opened one eye as she lay in her bed,
With a strange kind of thought going 'round in her head.
"You'd better get up," said the thought. "Check the clock!"
So she focused her gaze, and she got quite a shock.
Her digital timepiece said seven oh eight!
"I'm missing my school bus," thought Donna. "I'm late!"

Then she leaped out of bed in the dawn's early gloom,
And she tripped as she ran to her mom and dad's room.
"I'm going to be late! Please get up, Mom!" she cried.
But her mother just smiled and said, "Hey, look outside."
Donna looked . . . and her mouth and her eyes opened wide!

The scene that she saw was a Christmas tableau,
With the trees and the bushes all covered with snow,
And feathery flakes floating down to the ground,
Piling one on another with nary a sound.
"Good golly!" said Donna. "It's six inches deep!"
"No school," said her mother. "Now go back to sleep."

So Donna returned to the warmth of her bed,
But she just couldn't sleep. She was thinking instead,
Of all of the things she intended to do,
When she woke up again in an hour or two.

"Right after breakfast, I'll hurry outside,
With my sled," thought the girl, "and I'll go for a ride,
Down the hill all the way to the meadow and then,
I'll go back to the top and just zoom down again.
(I'm sure to go fast, but in case there's a doubt,
I'll soap up my runners before I go out.)

"I may even challenge Priscilla McGuire,
My friend up the street with the Flexible Flyer.
A championship race! Oh boy! What a thrill!
We'll speed like the wind, side by side down the hill,
And just as we get to the foot of the slope,
I'll pull ahead slightly (because of the soap)
And I'll win the big race by a whisker. (I hope.)

“The neighborhood kids are a cinch to be there,
With their breath making puffs of white smoke in the air.
And the boys will act weird and put on a big show,
As they stand with their sleds, till they see a girl go.
Then they’ll catch her and turn her sled into a drift.
(They won’t catch Priscilla or me . . . we’re too swift.)

"Some of the kids on the hill will be found,
Sledding on discs that keep spinning around.
Still others use carpets, and some kids, I know,
Will use plastic bags to slide down in the snow.
(Why, the last time it snowed, young Christopher Lantz
slid down the hill on the seat of his pants.)

“We’ll sled-ride all morning. Then, I’ve got a hunch,
That Priscilla might ask me to join her for lunch.
A cup of hot chocolate is ’specially nice,
Whenever your nose and your toes are like ice.
Then, after our mittens have warmed up and dried,
We’ll put on our parkas and head back outside.

"With two of us working it shouldn't be hard,
To build a snowman in Priscilla's front yard.
A SUPER-SIZED snowman, now, this'll be neat!
A huge seven-footer with gigantic feet!
We'll give him a nose that's as big as my fist,
And a grin on his face that is hard to resist.

“Well, what do you think? This is just the beginning.
Now we’ll show everyone why our snowman is grinning.
We’ll build him a snow wife and after she’s done,
We’ll keep right on going and build them a son.
(We’ll make him a snow kid licking a snow cone,
And petting a dog that is eating a snow bone.)

"We're not finished yet. Our work's not complete,
Until we prepare for the kids down the street.
The Ferguson brothers will see what we've done,
So they'll load up with snowballs and suddenly run,
Up the road with wild shouts as they start their attack
(and receive a surprise that will send them both back).

"We'll have built us a fort (like a three-sided wall),
All packed up with snow thirty-six inches tall,
And we'll crouch down inside. (We won't take a chance
We'll have two hundred snowballs all made in advance.)
We'll talk in a whisper, but this will all change,
As soon as the Fergusons get within range.

“What a great snowball fight! I can see it all now.
The Fergusons running up any old how,
And Priscilla and I with a great deal of poise,
Methodically pelting the Ferguson boys,
Till they’re covered with snow and their eyes are all blurry,
And they run down the street to their house in a hurry.

“So the Ferguson kids will go down in defeat,
And I will go home from Priscilla’s to eat.
Then, right after supper, before it gets dark,
I may take a walk with my dad near the park,
To look for the animal tracks in the snow.
(If you follow the tracks you can see where they go.)
We might track a possum or fox. Fancy that!
(Or it might be a neighborhood dog or a cat.)”

So these were the plans Donna made in her head,
As she lay snuggled down in the warmth of her bed.
Then her mother came in. Donna said, “Mom, you know,
There are many great things you can do in the snow.”
“Like what?” said her mom. So, before she went out,
Donna told her the things she’d been thinking about.

"You forgot one," said Mom, when she'd finished her talk.
"As soon as you eat, you can shovel the walk."

THE END